RORY
and his
Flying Friend

Author: Andrew Wolffe   Illustrator: Tom Cole

Text and illustrations copyright©, Keppel Publishing, 2003.
The Rory Stories is a Registered Trademark of Keppel Publishing.
This edition published 2003.
ISBN: 0 9534949 3 4

A CIP catalogue record for this book is available from the British Library.

Printed in Singapore

Keppel Publishing Ltd.
The Grey House, Kenbridge Road,
New Galloway, DG7 3RP, Scotland.

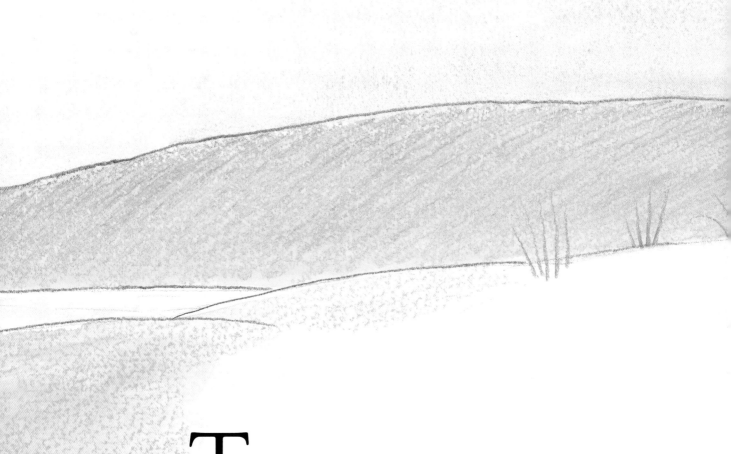

The sun shone brightly and, as usual, Rory and Scruff McDuff were having fun playing on the beach in Sandy Bay. Today, though, they felt too hot to do very much.

"I know," Rory said as he and Scruff McDuff strolled over the warm sand. "Let's go for a paddle."

The thought of splashing in the sea made Rory and Scruff McDuff pick up speed as they came closer to the water's edge. By the time they finally got there they had been walking so fast that they were both a little out of breath.

"The water will soon help you to cool down," Rory said as he patted Scruff McDuff, who was beginning to pant under his thick hairy coat.

Rory took off his sandshoes, tied them together by their laces, then hung them around his neck.

"Just in case they get wet or I lose them," he explained to a puzzled Scruff McDuff.

The water and soft sand felt pleasantly cool as they paddled in the sea.

"We can walk as far as those rocks over there then turn back," Rory suggested to Scruff McDuff.

The little dog was just about to wag his tail in agreement when they suddenly felt the sand beneath their feet tremble, twitch, then move from side to side. Before they knew what was happening, Rory and Scruff McDuff lost their balance...

...fell backwards...

...and landed in the water with an undignified PLOP!

Dripping wet, the little friends struggled to get back on their feet as the sand continued to move below them.

"Hold on tight Scruff McDuff, we're being lifted up in the air!" Rory shouted as the amazed pair began to rise out of the water.

"Well, I'm afraid that's what happens if you walk on top of me," said a voice from underneath them with a loud laugh.

Rory and Scruff McDuff looked down and discovered that they were sitting on top of a very large flat-fish who started to fly higher and higher up in the air.

"This is your captain speaking," the fish said. "Today we will be flying at an altitude high enough to get a good view but low enough to make an emergency landing, if the need arises."

T he fish gave another friendly smile to put his passengers at ease, then quickly dipped to one side to avoid a low-flying seagull.

"Looks like a learner to me," the fish said knowingly. "You always have to keep an eye out from them."

"Where are we going?" Rory asked, once he got over the surprise take off and began to enjoy the journey and the view.

"Wherever you like," the fish replied.

Rory looked around as they flew over the water below. "Can we fly past Captain Campbell's lighthouse?" he asked.

"Consider it done," the fish replied with a smile.

As the fish flew further up in the sky, Rory and Scruff McDuff leaned forward to make sure they didn't slide off his tail.

"Just sit back and relax," the fish soon advised his passengers. "I will now be maintaining a steady flight path until we reach our destination."

From up in the sky everything below seemed very far away and small. The cars parked beside Sandy Bay boat yard looked even smaller than Rory's toy ones, while the people walking along the cliffs were no more than tiny dots in the distance.

It seemed only a matter of minutes before the fish was approaching Sandy Bay's well known landmark.

"Look!" Rory exclaimed. "There's the lighthouse. We can see it flashing on and off every night to help the boats steer clear of the rocks."

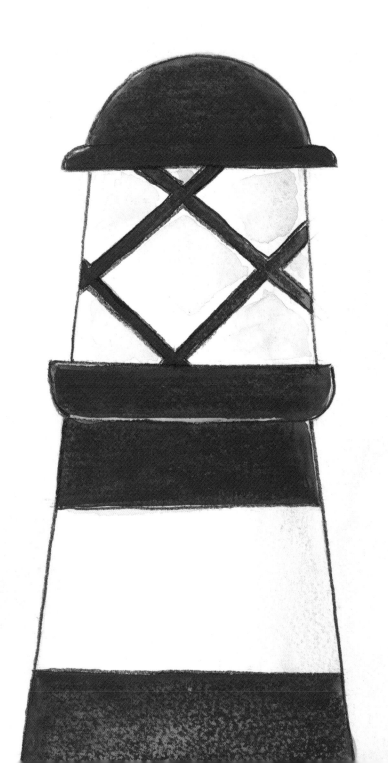

Having circled the lighthouse, the fish began to turn away and fly back to shore. Looking down, Rory suddenly spotted a small fishing boat stuck on the rocks and lying slightly on one side.

"I wonder if something is wrong?" Rory enquired. "Can we take a closer look?"

No sooner had Rory asked than the fish began to descend towards the rocks. As they drew nearer Rory could make out someone waving.

"It's Uncle Jack," Rory gasped as Scruff McDuff began to bark to say hello.

"There was a power cut in the lighthouse last night and I ran aground on the rocks," Uncle Jack shouted to Rory. "Can you fly back to Sandy Bay and ask the lifeboat to come and rescue me?"

Rory and Scruff McDuff felt very important when they arrived at the lifeboat station and explained what had happened to Uncle Jack.

"Well done Rory," said the lifeboat skipper. "We were beginning to worry because Jack's boat hadn't returned to harbour. Why don't you and Scruff McDuff come out with us in the lifeboat?"

So Rory was lucky enough to have two very exciting and very different trips in one day. Naturally, the fish didn't want to miss out on all the action. But this time he travelled the way fish normally do.